MONKEY
&ROBOT

Also by Peter Catalanotto
Daisy 1, 2, 3
Emily's Art
Ivan the Terrier
Kitten Red, Yellow, Blue
Matthew A.B.C.
Question Boy Meets Little Miss Know-It-All
More of Monkey & Robot

Monkey and Robot met at work.

MONKEY & ROBOT

by
PETER CATALANOTTO

A Richard Jackson Book

ATHENEUM BOOKS FOR YOUNG READERS
New York London Toronto Sydney New Delhi

To Chelsea

A
atheneum
ATHENEUM BOOKS FOR YOUNG READERS

An imprint of Simon & Schuster Children's Publishing Division 1230 Avenue of the Americas, New York, New York 10020 • This book is a work of fiction. Any references to historical events, real people, or real places are used fictitiously. Other names, characters, places, and events are products of the author's imagination, and any resemblance to actual events or places or persons, living or dead, is entirely coincidental. • Copyright © 2013 by Peter Catalanotto • All rights reserved, including the right of reproduction in whole or in part in any form. • ATHENEUM BOOKS FOR YOUNG READERS is a registered trademark of Simon & Schuster, Inc. • Atheneum logo is a trademark of Simon & Schuster, Inc. • For information about special discounts for bulk purchases, please contact Simon & Schuster Special Sales at 1-866-506-1949 or business@simonandschuster.com. • The Simon & Schuster Speakers Bureau can bring authors to your live event. For more information or to book an event, contact the Simon & Schuster Speakers Bureau at 1-866-248-3049 or visit our website at www.simonspeakers.com. • Also available in an Atheneum Books for Young Readers hardcover edition • Book design by Lauren Rille • The text for this book is set in Adobe Jensen Pro. • The illustrations for this book are rendered in pencil. • Manufactured in China • 0320 SCP • First Atheneum Books for Young Readers paperback edition June 2014 • 10 9 8 7 6 5 • The Library of Congress has cataloged the hardcover edition as follows: • Catalanotto, Peter. • Monkey and Robot / Peter Catalanotto. — 1st ed. • p. cm. • "A Richard Jackson book." • Summary: Best friends Monkey and Robot, who laugh and jump up and down when they are happy, enjoy a variety of activities. • ISBN 978-1-4424-2978-9 (hc) • ISBN 978-1-4424-3060-0 (eBook) • [1. Friendship—Fiction. 2. Robots—Fiction. 3. Monkeys—Fiction.] I. Title. • PZ7.C26878Mo 2013 • [E]—dc23 • 2012003044 • ISBN 978-1-4424-2979-6 (pbk)

CONTENTS

Monster Movie

"Do you want to watch a monster movie?" Robot asked.

"No," Monkey said. "They scare me."

"But it's fun," Robot said. "I like to be scared."

"I don't," Monkey said. "It's not fun to be scared. It's only scary."

"Let's try it," Robot said. "If you get scared, you can put the blanket over your head."

"Okay," Monkey said. He put the blanket over his head.

"The movie hasn't started yet," Robot said.

"I know," Monkey said. He took the blanket off his head. "I was just practicing."

Robot started the movie.

Monkey screamed and put the blanket over his head. "Stop the movie!" he said.

Robot stopped the movie. "What's the matter?"

"I remembered something really scary from the last scary movie I watched," Monkey said.

"What was it?" Robot asked.

"I told you," Monkey said. "Something really scary."

"Oh," Robot said. "Would you like some popcorn?"

"Yes!" Monkey said. He took the blanket off his head. "I love popcorn."

Robot walked to the kitchen and put some popcorn into a bowl. When he came back into the living room, Monkey screamed and put his head under the blanket.

"What's the matter now?" Robot asked.

"That is the bowl I ate popcorn from when I saw the really scary something that I just remembered before!" Monkey said.

Robot walked back to the kitchen and put the popcorn into a different bowl. When he returned to the living room, Monkey still had the blanket over his head.

"Are you going to keep the blanket over your head for the entire movie?" Robot asked.

"Yes," Monkey said. "I think I should."

Robot turned the movie back on and sat next to Monkey.

Monkey screamed. Robot turned off the movie.

"Now what's the matter?" Robot asked.

"The music from this movie is very scary," Monkey said.

"Whenever you hear something scary, just hum," Robot said.

Monkey started to hum.

"Are you going to hum for the entire movie?" Robot asked.

"I . . . hmm . . . think . . . hmm . . . I . . . hmm . . . should," Monkey said.

Robot turned on the movie.

Monkey ate popcorn and hummed with the blanket over his head for the entire movie.

"The movie is over," Robot said.

Monkey stopped humming and took the blanket off his head. "That was the best monster movie I ever saw," he said.

Robot looked at Monkey. "Scary things in movies aren't real," he said.

Monkey looked down at the empty bowl.

"The monster in that movie isn't real," Robot said.

Monkey thought about that.

"And the blood in that movie isn't real either," Robot said.

Monkey thought about that, too. Then he said, "I know the monster in the movie isn't real. And I know the blood in the movie isn't real. But do you know what is *really* real?"

"What?" Robot asked.

"That I really get really scared at monster movies," Monkey said.

"Okay," Robot said. "What would you like to do now?"

"Let's watch another monster movie!" Monkey said. He put the blanket over his head and started to hum. Robot went into the kitchen and filled the bowl with popcorn.

The Game

"Do you want to play a game?" Robot asked.

"No," Monkey said. "I don't like to lose."

"But you might win," Robot said.

"Oh, I know," Monkey said, "but I don't like to win, either. If I win, then I'll feel bad that you lost."

"Hmm," Robot said. "But I won't feel bad if I lose. I just like to play."

"I wish I could be like that," Monkey said.

"Could you try?" Robot asked. "Could you try and play just for the fun of it?"

"Just for fun?" Monkey asked.

"Yes," Robot said. "A nice, friendly, fun game."

"Okay," Monkey said. "Please pass me the dice."

"Die," Robot said. Monkey started to cry.

"What's the matter?" Robot asked.

"You said we would have a nice, friendly, fun game," Monkey said.

"We will!" Robot said.

"But you just told me to die. That's not nice, friendly, or fun!"

"I didn't tell you to die," Robot said. "That's what *this* is called. Two are called 'dice,' but one is called 'a die.'"

"Oh," Monkey said. He cupped his hands around the die and shook it. He shook really hard. The die popped out of his hands and flew out the window.

"Oh dear," Robot said. He looked outside. "I see it! You got a five!"

A dog ran into the yard and picked up the die.

"I'll get it!" Monkey yelled. When the dog saw Monkey, it started to run around the yard. The ground was very muddy. Monkey tried to catch the dog, but he slipped and fell. Robot laughed. The dog dropped the die.

"It's a four!" Monkey yelled. He tried to grab the die, but the dog picked it up and ran away again. Monkey chased the dog and slipped and fell again. Robot laughed again.

"Drop it!" Monkey yelled. The dog dropped the die.

"It's a two!" Monkey yelled. The dog picked up the die again, and Monkey chased it and fell again. Robot laughed even harder.

The dog dropped the die.

"It's a six!" Monkey yelled. The dog kept picking up the die and dropping the die. Monkey kept chasing the dog and falling. Robot kept laughing.

"It's a three!" Monkey yelled. "It's a one! A five! A two! A five! A three! Six! One! Three!"

Finally the dog dropped the die and lay down.

"Four!" Monkey yelled. He dove and grabbed the die. "I got it!"

Robot's tummy hurt from laughing so hard. "Well," he said, "on your first turn you got a five, a four, a two, a six, a three, a one, a five, a two, another five, a three, a six, a one, a three, and a four."

"How much is that?" asked Monkey. The dog licked his face.

"Fifty," Robot said. He moved Monkey's playing piece fifty times. It went all the way to the last space on the board.

"You win!" Robot shouted.

Monkey walked into the house. He was covered with mud. "Are you sad?"

When Robot saw Monkey, he started laughing again. "No," he said. "That was the most fun I ever had playing a game."

"I'm glad," Monkey said. "After I take a bath we should play again."

"Yes," Robot said. "We should."

The Cocoon

"What's on this stick?" Monkey asked.

"A cocoon," Robot said.

"It looks like a tiny sleeping bag," Monkey said.

"It is," Robot said. "A caterpillar made that cocoon and is sleeping in there right now."

"Wow," said Monkey. "When will it wake up and come out?"

"Soon," Robot said. "Let's take it home. You will be amazed by how different the caterpillar will look when it comes out."

"Will the caterpillar have a beard?" Monkey asked.

"No," Robot said.

Robot and Monkey went home. Robot set an empty fish tank on the window ledge in Monkey's room.

"Is the caterpillar going to turn into a fish?" Monkey asked.

"No," Robot said. He placed the stick with the cocoon in the fish tank. Then he put a screen on top of the fish tank.

"Can I peek into the cocoon?" Monkey asked.

"No," Robot said. "The caterpillar is still changing."

"So the caterpillar is naked right now?" Monkey asked.

"Just wait until it comes out," Robot said. "You will be very surprised."

"What if the caterpillar is hungry when it comes out?" Monkey asked.

"We can put some leaves and grass in the tank," Robot said. "That will also make the tank look pretty."

Robot and Monkey gathered leaves and grass and placed it into the fish tank. Robot yawned. "It's late," he said. "Time for bed."

Monkey went to bed, but he could not sleep. He was too excited. He got up and looked at the cocoon.

"Leaves and grass look pretty," Monkey said, "but leaves and grass are boring to eat."

Monkey went into the kitchen and made a peanut-butter-and-banana sandwich. He cut the sandwich into four pieces and put them into the fish tank. "That's better," he said. Monkey got back into bed and closed his eyes. He fell asleep.

A squirrel hopped onto the window ledge and knocked the cover off the fish tank. It grabbed a piece of the sandwich. Monkey woke up. He saw the squirrel and screamed. The squirrel ran away. Monkey ran into Robot's room.

"Robot! Robot!" Monkey yelled. "The caterpillar turned into a squirrel!"

"Caterpillars do not turn into squirrels," Robot said. "You must have been dreaming."

Monkey walked back into his room. He looked at the fish tank. He saw the cocoon. "Hmm," Monkey said. "I guess I was dreaming." He went back to bed.

A raccoon jumped onto the window ledge. It grabbed a piece of the sandwich. Monkey sat up. He saw the raccoon and screamed. The raccoon ran away. Monkey ran into Robot's room.

"Robot! Robot!" Monkey yelled. "The caterpillar turned into a raccoon!"

Robot sat up. "Caterpillars do not turn into raccoons," he said. "You were dreaming again!"

Monkey walked back into his room. He
saw the cocoon in the fish tank. He scratched
his head. "Robot was right," he said. "I was
dreaming again." Monkey climbed into bed.

A bear climbed up onto the window ledge and grabbed the rest of the sandwich. Monkey sat up. He saw the bear and screamed. The bear ran away. Monkey ran into Robot's room.

"Robot! Robot!" Monkey yelled. "The caterpillar turned into a bear!"

Robot jumped out of bed. They ran back to Monkey's room. The cocoon was still on the stick. "Caterpillars don't turn into bears," Robot said. Monkey noticed the peanut-butter-and-banana sandwich was gone.

"The naked caterpillar came out and ate a whole sandwich!" Monkey said.

"No, it didn't," Robot said. "You were dreaming." He put the cover back on the fish tank.

"May I sleep in your room and you sleep in my room?" Monkey asked.

"Okay," Robot said.

Monkey went into Robot's room and got into bed. He wondered what the caterpillar would turn into after eating a whole sandwich. A rhinoceros? An elephant? A dinosaur? Monkey fell asleep.

The next morning Robot was very excited. "Wake up! Wake up!" he said. "The caterpillar came out of the cocoon!"

Monkey ran to his bedroom to see the big surprise. He looked around. He did not see any giant animals.

"Look in the fish tank!" Robot said. Monkey looked in the fish tank. He saw a moth fluttering around. "Isn't it amazing?" Robot asked.

"That's it?" Monkey asked. "A bug?"

"A moth," Robot said. "What were you expecting, a hippopotamus?"

Monkey climbed into his own bed. "No," he said. "Don't be ridiculous. I *never* thought the caterpillar would turn into a hippopotamus." Monkey put his head under the covers. Robot took the top off the tank. He watched the moth fly away.

Hide-and-Seek

"Do you want to play hide-and-seek?" Monkey asked.

"Okay," Robot said, "but I don't know how to play."

"It's easy," Monkey said. "I'll count to fifty while you go someplace where I can't see you. When I'm finished counting I'll yell, 'ready or not, here I come,' and then I'll look for you."

"What happens when you find me?" Robot asked.

"We hug and laugh and jump up and down," Monkey said.

"That sounds wonderful," Robot said.

"It is," Monkey said. "Okay, I'm going to start counting."

Monkey sat at the table, folded his arms, and lay down his head. He started to count. Robot walked behind Monkey and waited quietly.

". . . Forty-seven," Monkey said, "forty-eight, forty-nine, *fifty!*"

Monkey sat up. When he turned and saw Robot, he shrieked and fell off his chair. Robot helped Monkey up. He asked, "Are you okay?"

"You scared me," Monkey said.

"I wanted to hide near you, so you would find me right away and we could hug and laugh and jump up and down," Robot said.

"Okay," Monkey said. He hugged Robot. They laughed and jumped up and down.

"Now," Monkey said, "I'll count again, but this time you go hide somewhere else."

"What happens if you don't find me?" Robot asked.

"I don't know," Monkey said. "But don't worry, I will."

Monkey put his head back down on the table and started counting to fifty. Robot went and hid. When Monkey finished counting he yelled, "Ready or not, here I come!"

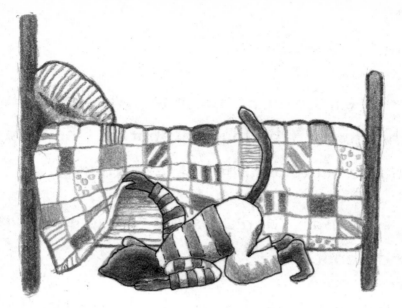

Monkey looked under the kitchen table. Then he looked in the living room. He looked under the beds and behind the drapes. He even looked in the bathtub. Monkey couldn't find Robot anywhere.

He sat down on the floor. Monkey knew what to do if he found Robot, but he didn't know what to do if he didn't find him.

"Oh dear," Monkey said. "What if I *never* find Robot."

Monkey looked at the kitchen table. "If I don't find Robot, we'll never dunk cookies in milk together again," he said.

Monkey looked at the easel. "If I don't find Robot, we'll never draw pictures together again," he said.

Monkey looked at the couch. "If I don't find Robot, we'll never watch movies together again," he said.

Monkey started to cry. "I can't live here without Robot," he said. "I miss him so much. I must find somewhere else to live."

He walked slowly to the closet to get his coat. When Monkey opened the door and saw Robot, he shrieked and fell to the floor. Robot helped him up.

"Are you okay?" Robot asked.

"Why did you leave?" Monkey asked. "Were you mad at me?"

"No," Robot said. "I was hiding and waiting for you to find me."

Monkey wiped his nose. "Did you miss me?" he asked.

"Very much," Robot said. "I couldn't wait for you to find me."

Monkey hugged Robot.

"You shrieked when you found me right away," Robot said. "And you shrieked when it took you a long time to find me."

Monkey nodded his head.

"Maybe this game should be called hide-and-shriek," Robot said.

"Maybe it should," Monkey said.

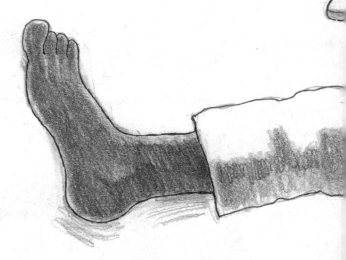

Then they laughed and jumped up and down.